Joe's Bible

A Teen's Journey to Salvation

Joe's Bible

A Teen's Journey to Salvation

TJ Martini

JOE'S BIBLE
by TJ Martini

© Copyright 2002 by TJ Martini
First Printing January 2003

Layout and Design, Jay Degn, *Reno, Nevada*
Editor, Leah Witt, *Reno, Nevada*
Concept, Gary Lebeck, *Reno, Nevada*

Photographs of Ashley Oliveira on Cover and Title page:
Jeff Spicer, *Spicer Photography, Reno, Nevada ~ www.jeffspicer.com*

Foreword photo of Parks Bonifay: Courtesy of Bonifay Family
Pages 7, 52-59: Courtesy of Paul and Joan Scafidi

Scripture quotations, New International Version (NIV) Bible

WingsNV Publishing

Printed in the United States of America
By Walsworth Publishing Company, Marceline, Missouri

ISBN 0–9705018–9–7

Library of Congress Cataloging–in–Publication Data
Martini, T. J., 1948–
Joe's Bible A Teen's Journey to Salvation / T.J. Martini.
    p. cm.
ISBN 0–9705018–9–7
I. Title.
PS3613.A787 J64 2003
813'.6—dc21

                                    2002153370

FOR JOE & DAN

IN HEARTFELT GRATITUDE...

This book is lovingly dedicated to the two
strongest people I have ever known,
Paul and Joan Scafidi, in the precious
memories of their sons, Daniel and Joseph.

When Paul and Joan first got the news that both
of their boys had been killed, they could have so
easily given up and walked away, but they didn't.
They could have pointed a hateful finger toward
God for the untimely loss of their only children,
but not once did this ever cross their minds.
To this day they remain faithful,
loyal and dedicated Christians.

Their marriage is a testimony in itself to the Lord, for it is through Him that they find their incredible courage and strength. I admire them both tremendously for their determination to continue to spread the word of Jesus Christ with open, willing and grateful hearts no matter what His will may be.

Paul and Joan, I want to thank you for allowing me the honor and the privilege of telling the world about your amazing walk with Jesus, first as a family with your precious children, and now, in your determined yet much harder walk without them.

God is watching you, my friends, and He is very proud. Someday you will both surely hear the words, "Well done, thou good and faithful servants!"

God bless you, now and for eternity,

PJ Martini

FOREWORD
By Parks Bonifay
World Cup Champion Wakeboarder 2001

When I first received the request to write this Foreword I had just lost a close friend in a freak motorcycle accident. I remembered thinking at the time how short life really is, and how it can be taken away so quickly, without any warning at all. When I was told how much Joe Scafidi loved to "board" I knew that I wanted to be a part of this book. I actually remember Joe when I was doing a personal appearance in Reno and he approached me to sign his poster. His smile was unforgettable, and he was so eager and full of life. He was a true "boarder" in all aspects and a very grateful fan.

I began skiing at Cypress Gardens at the tender age of two and worked a 30–hour week by the time I was seven. For the next five years I did tournament after tournament. During these years I had many professional skiers whom I admired. I dreamed that one day I would be just like them. Like Joe, I had pictures of them all over my bedroom walls. They were so gracious and always took the time to answer questions and sign autographs for me.

Now that I am in the spotlight I try to do the same. I know how important the fans are to a professional athlete and I will always take the time to answer questions and sign autographs. It pleases me greatly to see people enjoying what I love to do the most.

I was extremely saddened to hear that Joe had been killed in a car accident along with his older brother. He was so young. My deepest regrets go out to his family and friends.

There are just no guarantees that any of us will be able to live out our dreams and passions, but I know we should always try. I want to take this opportunity to thank all my fans for their support and to tell them to never give up. I'm sure that had Joe been given more time, he very well could have been signing autographs for his own fans! His parents should be very proud.

(Parks Bonifay began wakeboarding in 1996 and was Pro Tour Champion for 2001–2002. He also won the Big Air Tournament Masters in 2002, at Callaway Gardens in Florida. Parks was Joe Scafidi's hero, someone he looked up to and hoped to be like one day. My deepest gratitude to Parks for taking the time to acknowledge Joe, as well as to lend encouragement and support to his many other fans all over the world.)

Joe's Bible

A TEEN'S JOURNEY TO SALVATION

CHAPTER 1
SATURDAY,
DECEMBER 15, 2001
11:15 PM

Dear Diary:

"Before I woke up this morning I could honestly say that I had never really known anyone that had died. But I can't say that now, not anymore. Today one of my best friends was in a car accident and died alongside his brother. He was only 14. His name was Joe.

"People are always telling me that God has a plan for everyone, and I have always believed this. I believe His plan for me is to do well in high school, go to college, graduate and be happy in my life; that is, assuming my life will extend past my freshman year and throughout my adulthood. But it didn't happen that way for Joe or for his brother Dan, who had just turned 18 in September.

"Today, all the dreams that Joe and Dan had for their futures don't really matter anymore. Maybe I shouldn't be questioning God's motives, but if taking two young boys from us was a good plan, I can't help but wonder what's in store for me and for the rest of us who are left behind.

> AND WHAT MAKES 14 AND 18 YEARS OLD THE RIGHT TIME TO DIE?

"'Everything happens for a reason,' people say. Or, 'It must have been their time.' Is all of this supposed to make me feel better? It doesn't exactly help me cope. And what about their parents? It makes no sense to me that the only children they had were taken from them today. Where is the reasoning in this? And what makes 14 and 18 years old the right time to die?

"Now people are going to tell me that 'Joe is in a better place' and 'He isn't feeling any pain,' which I really hope is true. I keep telling myself over and over that Joe is gone forever. But I don't know if I will ever really believe it. How can he be? He was so young. But for now there's nothing I can do, except pray. Not for Joe or Dan, because I want so much to believe that they are all right, but for their loved ones who aren't in a better place yet and are still feeling pain—a whole lot of it. These are the people who need love and support right now because this may be the hardest obstacle they will ever have to face. Help them through this time of loss and sorrow, God. At a time like this, no one wants to feel alone.

"I have to close now, diary and try to get some sleep. Thank you for listening and being a friend. Like always, Ashley."

When she finished writing down her painful thoughts, Ashley didn't feel better liked she had hoped. She crawled into the safe haven of her queen–size bed and wrapped herself tightly in the comforter that was spread across the top. She cried, she prayed, she died a little herself that day. Ashley was still in shock from the news she heard earlier that evening. She knew she would be for a very long time.

CHAPTER 2
MONDAY,
DECEMBER 17, 2001
6:50 AM

Young Ashley Oliveira poked her head out from beneath the covers and looked out her bedroom window just as the sun began its day. Once again she thought about her friend. Her heart ached, as the memory of Joe's smile passed through her mind for the hundredth time since he was killed just two days before. Had it only been two days? Her confusion was still so evident. She couldn't hide the fact that she questioned God's reasons for what seemed to be such an unnecessary, cruel and untimely accident that killed her friend and his older brother. God could have stopped it if He wanted, couldn't He? After all, He is God and He can do anything. Or so she used to believe. But now she wasn't so sure. If He was such a good God, a caring God, how could He let this kind of thing happen, especially to someone so kind and so undeserving as Joe?

Over and over Ashley cried out into her pillow to muffle the sounds of her pain, "Why Joe?" He was so young, and his kind and caring heart was as big as he was. It all seemed so senseless.

Not wanting to leave the comfort of her bed too quickly, Ashley glanced over at the clock and realized it was almost time to get up. She slowly unwrapped herself from the covers and headed for the shower. It was Monday, another school day and, like it or not, she had to get ready.

It began like any other school day for the petite young freshman, as she hurried through her morning routine. But this day would be more different than any other Ashley had ever known. This day one of her best friends would be missing. Joe wouldn't be there as he had been nearly every day for the past five years. It would be hard to concentrate on her studies, as she looked at the empty chair next to hers, knowing she would never again see Joe sitting there.

For nearly five years he made her laugh with his little jokes and mischievous ways—things he usually got away with more so than most of the other kids. But Joe never hurt anyone intentionally. He didn't have a mean bone in his entire body and he just seemed to sparkle no matter what he was doing, right or wrong. Ashley believed Joe got away with more because he was so cute with his sky–blue eyes and snow–blonde hair, and rather small stature, standing just barely five feet tall. His size never seemed to bother him, though; Joe knew that someday he would grow to at least as tall as his brother and his dad, maybe even taller. But not now. Joe would always be just five feet tall.

After Ashley was dressed her father, Chuck, dropped her off at the usual place in the side parking lot at Reno High. She walked the long path up to the entrance of the school and opened the double doors. As she entered, the mood was oppressive, even to those who didn't know Joe and Dan. Even the walls seemed a shade or two darker, as if they knew this day would be different for everyone who cried at the loss of their friends and fellow students. Dan graduated from Reno High School and his little brother, Joe, was just a freshman. Their accident and deaths were the talk of the school and the subject of nearly every class.

For those who hadn't already heard about the boys, rumors spread quickly that two of their own had died over the weekend. Sobs echoed from one end of the building to the other, from girls and boys, as well as many adults and teachers. There wasn't anyone that wasn't touched by the loss. It was a long, sad day for Ashley, and one she would never forget.

Dan had just started his first year at college. He had just been accepted on a full tennis and academic scholarship at St. Mary's College in Northern California and was well on his way to becoming a professional tennis player.

The year before Dan had won the Nevada State High School Singles' Tennis Championship, following in one of his heroes, that of Andre Agassi, who won the Nevada title in 1988 from Las Vegas. After taking his final exams at St. Mary's the week before, Dan was looking forward to a well–deserved winter break and had just driven home to Reno that Friday.

Everyone was talking about the accident, about how the boys died together, and how it seemed fitting because they were so close. Ashley didn't know Dan very well, only through being friends with Joe and going to his house on occasion when Dan was there. And now they were gone, both of them at the same time. Talk about unfair!

Later that same afternoon, the Freshman Football
Team that Joe had played on earlier that fall, hung
posters and passed out flyers all around the school
letting everyone know that a vigil in remembrance
of both boys was planned for seven o'clock that
evening. Word spread quickly, and many of the students
made plans to attend. Ashley and several of her close
girlfriends knew they wouldn't miss it for the world.
The day dragged on for all of them.

Several of the young freshmen girls, including
Ashley, were on the Junior Varsity Cheer Team and
had a practice right after school. It was hard for them
to stay focused and to concentrate as they practiced
their routines. All three of the Reno High cheer squads
were affected by the boys' passing, but they managed
to continue, though for many,
the mystery and uncertainty of
death would never again be
quite so distant.

> THE DARKENED
> SKIES SHINED
> BRIGHT FROM THE
> LIGHT OF CANDLES
> BURNING IN THE
> STUDENTS' HANDS,
> HUNDREDS WITHIN
> A TWO—BLOCK
> RADIUS

Most of Joe's freshmen
classmates, along with many of
the upper classmen who knew
both boys, attended the vigil
which was held outside the
brothers' home. It was a sight

to be seen! The darkened skies shined bright from the light of candles burning in the students' hands, hundreds within a two–block radius.

The view from the porch was a breathtaking miracle and an answer to many prayers for Joan and Paul Scafidi, Joe and Dan's parents. That night they witnessed hundreds of young faces, with noses running and cheeks streaming with tears, as they stopped by to pay their last respects, and to hopefully bring a small dose of comfort to the parents of their dear friends. Occasionally a sob or a moan was heard in the distance, which echoed through the still night air as the crowd began singing "Silent Night." From their doorway, Joan and Paul watched in heartfelt gratitude. Never before had they been so touched by such an outpouring of complete and utter love and compassion.

One face, however, stood out more than the others, as she slowly worked her way toward the front of the house. It was Ashley. She needed to hear first hand that her precious Joey was really gone. She searched the crowd for familiar eyes, comforting eyes, knowing eyes, and at last she made contact. Tears and mascara streamed down her cheeks as she looked into the faces of Joe's mother and father. The truth suddenly became painfully clear as it rang in her ears and tore at her broken heart. Joe was gone forever.

"How can such a good God be so cruel? How will I ever understand any of this?" Ashley cried to herself as she inched her way forward. "And what about poor Paul and Joan? The boys were all they had. In one split second their entire family was taken from them. How can they ever accept the senselessness of it all? How could anyone?"

Ashley finally reached Joan and collapsed into her open arms for a comfort she knew would be hard to find. "How selfish is this?" Ashley cried out. "I should be trying to comfort you and I don't know how. Please, tell me what I can do? Show me how to make it good for you again."

Looking deep into Joan's eyes, Ashley waited for a response. It came slowly, but it was surprisingly calm. "There is nothing anyone can do, sweetie. It's so hard for us to believe that our boys are really gone. But I am comforted knowing they are together and at peace with our Lord."

Ashley couldn't believe what she was hearing! Where were the sobs, the tragic cries for help? Shouldn't Joan be falling apart? They were her kids. Her only kids. Doesn't she know she will never see them again? How can she be so strong? And look at Paul, their dad. He seems so calm, almost surreal.

Don't they get it? Their sons are dead! How do
they hide their pain and pretend it isn't killing them
inside? "Tell me how you guys do it so I can do it
too?" she begged silently, but to no avail. The longer she
stayed and observed, the more confused and troubled
she became.

CHAPTER 3
TUESDAY,
DECEMBER 18, 2001
3:00 PM

After school had ended, Ashley once again focused on her cheerleading and being at the basketball games. It seemed to be the only time she wasn't thinking about Joe. Needless to say, cheering became her center of attention and her focus for survival. Everything else seemed to remind her of him. But Joe never played basketball. So being on the basketball court wasn't too bad.

The crowd was pumped and the cheerleaders and basketball players fed off their energy. The girls were louder than usual as they led the spirited audience into dozens of chants and cheers. The walls of the gymnasium vibrated with enthusiasm and excitement from all directions. Several hours later when the games came to a close, silence filled the room once again.

> TEARS SOAKED HER PILLOW AND WHAT WAS LEFT OF HER SHATTERED HEART CONTINUED TO BREAK INTO TINY FRAGMENTS

It was an evening to celebrate for both the boys' and girls' basketball teams. They were still undefeated. The cheerleaders joined in the celebration and laughter and Ashley tried her best to enjoy the victory. But when several of the girls wanted to go for pizza afterward, Ashley declined, claiming instead to be too tired. She walked outside and waited for her dad.

On the drive home, she asked him if she could go to Grace Community Church on Saturday night with one of the girls from her squad. Kara Werner, who was the Junior Varsity Captain and more than two years older than Ashley, had been talking to several of the girls about her church since the beginning of the year. Ashley thought it might be a good time to go and check it out. She had high hopes that maybe she could find some answers there.

As she readied herself for bed, her thoughts immediately went to Joe. Tears soaked her pillow and what was left of her shattered heart continued to break into tiny fragments. Ashley wondered how much more she could take. She was exhausted, depressed, confused and in more pain than she had ever known before. For hours she lay there and watched the clock on her radio, as the night turned slowly into dawn. If only she could pretend that all was as it was before Saturday, before the accident, before the phone call. If only…

Chapter 4
WEDNESDAY,
DECEMBER 19, 2001
8:00 AM

The halls were once again abuzz with the boy's accident and the site where they were killed. The site had already been visited by hundreds of students from all different schools in the area. Some paid their last respects; others, who had never met the boys, were just curious about how and where it happened, following several articles that had appeared in the newspaper and on television.

Now the small dirt area on the side of the highway, where the truck ran off and flipped over, was smothered in cards, notes and stuffed animals, as well as dozens of flowers from well–wishers all around the city. A family friend had also put up two white metal crosses inscribed with each of the boys' names. Ashley had visited the memorial site the night before and remembered hearing how the accident happened.

Dan had been driving late that Saturday afternoon while Joe was nestled comfortably in the passenger's seat. Both boys were wearing their seatbelts. The weather was cold but clear as the sun began to set behind the mountain, creating a golden sunset on the horizon. The boys spent the entire day skiing and snowboarding together. By the time they headed for home, they were both exhausted, especially Dan. He hadn't slept very well for several weeks due to his grueling schedule at school with his final exams. He planned to make up for the lack of sleep when he got home for winter break, but not until after the planned ski trip. Though Dan had lost interest in skiing and hadn't gone in several years, he was looking forward to being with Joe, along with some of his friends from school. He spent the next several hours skiing and bonding with his little brother. Because Joe was a snowboarder, Dan stayed on the lower part of the mountain to be closer to him. They rode the ski lift together several times, and Joe was rarely out of Dan's sight.

According to the police report, Dan was even more tired than he knew. It only took a mere three seconds and their world changed forever, just long enough to cross the center divide into the oncoming traffic; a single car heading up the hill. A few of Dan's friends were following close behind and saw him drifting across several lanes of the highway. They tried desperately to get his attention by honking their horns and yelling out the window, but he never heard them.

Dan never knew what happened. If he had, he would never have forgiven himself. On the drive home that late sunny afternoon around five o'clock, with his younger brother sleeping beside him, the always-dependable and always-responsible Dan Scafidi fell asleep at the wheel.

Ashley knew she would never understand the senselessness of it all. If there were ever two boys that were meant to live full and successful lives, it was Dan and Joe. They had so much going for them and so much to live for. Surely they could have changed many lives had they been given the chance. But it was not to be.

> IF THERE WERE EVER TWO BOYS THAT WERE MEANT TO LIVE FULL AND SUCCESSFUL LIVES, IT WAS DAN AND JOE

Ashley's lack of sleep soon began to take its toll. Her eyes weren't as bright as they usually were, nor was her heart. The bounce that was in her step was gone and her spirit was broken. The normally happy cheerleader, to whom everyone was drawn by her outgoing nature and cheerful smile, didn't show up this day. No one was sure if she ever would again.

Even through her heartache, Ashley soon realized that no matter what the circumstance, life still went on. After school the cheerleaders had yet another practice and Ashley was expected to be there. She was a tumbler and a flyer on the squad, and because she was so petite, she did it well. As she walked down the hall toward the practice area, confusion and pain covered her face like a veil.

CHAPTER 5
THURSDAY,
DECEMBER 20, 2001
11:45 AM

The boys' memorial service was scheduled for two o'clock. Because Joe and Dan were both so well–known and liked, all the junior high and high schools in the area shortened the classes, enabling all the students to attend the service.

Ashley arrived early with her best friends and fellow cheerleaders Jenny Luna and Cathy Strand, as the First Evangelical Free Church of Reno began to fill to capacity…and then some. The music played and many of the guests began singing the familiar Christian songs while lifting their hands high in the air, as if reaching for comfort from above. After several songs, Pastor Tony Slavin, a family friend from Grace Community Church in Reno, took his place at the podium.

41

He spoke highly of both boys and their parents, of how Joe and Dan were raised, and of the accident that took them away. Then he bowed his head and said a prayer. When he was through, Pastor Tony said a few words on Joan and Paul's behalf before they came up to speak.

> BECAUSE OF THE LORD'S GREAT LOVE, WE ARE NOT CONSUMED, FOR HIS COMPASSIONS NEVER FAIL

"Paul and Joan want to thank each and every one of you for your compassion and kindness to them as they grieve the loss of their children…you have been Jesus' hands and feet to them. They also want to thank God, their Father, for supplying the strength to get them through the next few minutes. In their desire to share the hope that sustains them, they invite you to meditate on these Scriptures as we remember their children.

'I am poured out like water, and all my bones are out of joint. My heart has turned to wax; it has melted away within me.' Psalm 22:14

'Because of the Lord's great love, we are not consumed, for His compassions never fail. They are new every morning; great is Your faithfulness.' Lamentations 3:22,23

'Humble yourselves therefore under the mighty hand of God, that He may exalt you in due time: Casting all your cares upon Him; for He careth for you.' 1 Peter 5:6,7

'The Lord appeared to us in the past, saying: "I have loved you with an everlasting love; I have drawn you with loving–kindness."' Jeremiah 31:3

'Now we see but a poor reflection as in a mirror; then we shall see face to face. Now I know in part; then I shall know fully, even as I am fully known. And now these three remain; faith, hope and love. But the greatest of these is love.' 1 Corinthians 13:12,13

'…I know He will rise again in the resurrection of the last day.' Jesus said, 'I am the Resurrection and the Life. He who believes in Me will live, even though he dies; and whoever lives and believes in Me will never die. Do you believe this?'" John 11:24–26

After the last of the Scriptures was read, Pastor Tony left the stage just as Paul and Joan entered. Silence filled the room, and the grieving couple approached the podium to begin telling their story to the more than one thousand people in attendance. Paul did most of the talking, while Joan stood at her husband's side, encouraging and supporting him as she had done for nearly 20 years.

"When tragedy like this happens, your choices are fairly simple. You can curl up and die, or you can carry on and live. If you choose life, you can either live in tragedy or in victory. Joan and I have chosen victory. The temptation to get angry and blame God under these circumstances is very real. But I am here to tell all of you that not for a second has that thought entered either of our minds. Instead, we have been praying for grateful hearts. Hearts that overflow with joy at the honor God gave us to raise two of the most beautiful people ever to grace this planet. As their father, you all would expect me to say this. But all you need to do is look around this room to see that what I say is true."

> THEY BOTH SHOWED TREMENDOUS STRENGTH AND GAVE ALL THE CREDIT TO A LOVING AND MERCIFUL GOD

Ashley was moved to tears, as was everyone, by the faith which Paul and Joan displayed. They were drawing on their belief that God was good and that He would never leave them, especially in their incredible time of need. They both showed tremendous strength and gave all the credit to a loving and merciful God, thanking Him for helping them through this horrendous ordeal, knowing they could never do it without Him. They held each other for support. They talked, but they never broke down. They cried, but they never lost their composure. Everyone's eyes were on the pair, as if mesmerized by the comfort in their voices.

From the third row Ashley listened, unable to take her eyes away from the couple even for a moment. She was not only touched but also extremely amazed. She wondered once again how they remained so focused and unbelievably strong!

"Throughout this week the heartache has been unimaginable," Paul continued tearfully. "But within the tragedy, God has moved mightily. On Monday night He sent close to 300 people to our home to minister to us. Anyone that was there will tell you that it was the most beautiful outpouring of love they had ever witnessed. All week He has sent a continual stream of people to our home with flowers, fond memories of our children, love, and affection. And last night I received a phone call from Craig Berg, who is the gentleman that my children hit on Saturday night. He called to tell us how sorry he was for our loss. He also said that he wanted to plant two trees in our garden, as a living memorial to our boys. His kindness last night lifted a burden from our shoulders that you can't imagine. Joan and I have cried out to God in anguish everyday, and He has shown His love through the arms of all of you. We can't thank you enough."

Paul glanced down at his notes as he began to tell the crowded sanctuary a few stories about each of his boys, ones that made them unique and special in their own right. Some were amusing as they showed just how different the brothers were, while other stories touched deeply at the heart.

"Daniel and Joseph were both kind, loving and had great senses of humor, especially Joseph. Daniel was disciplined, thoughtful, and heading into a bright future with great purpose. Joseph was not disciplined, a bit of a clown, extremely creative and heading into a bright future with little purpose. They both would have ended up in a similar place but taken very different routes.

"Throughout his early years, Daniel worked very hard in studies and tennis in order to get a scholarship to one of the finer colleges. That college turned out to be St. Mary's. As you all know, college tuition is expensive and even with Daniel's tennis scholarship, it would have been a struggle to send him. I told him not to worry about the tuition, that my toy budget would just have to be put on hold for four years.

"One day after returning from work, I noticed a letter hanging from my office door. It was a congratulatory letter to Daniel for winning the Presidential Scholarship, which just about covered his whole tuition! At the bottom of the letter Daniel wrote, 'Dad, you're back in the toy business!' I can remember running around the house hugging anything that was standing still." The church filled with laughter, and Paul and Joan's eyes filled with tears at the memory of that special day.

"And then there's Joseph with his pink hair," Paul said smiling, as his face lit up with the thought of his youngest child. The story he told about Joe was one of Ashley's favorites.

"It happened one day when Joan and I were out of town. We let Joe stay with one of his friends, while Dan stayed at the house. The first evening they spent together, Joe and his friend, Nick Peele, decided they wanted to put red streaks in their hair. Nick was as dark as Joe was blonde.

"They bought the package of color at the drug store and each one did the other's hair. When they were through, Nick had streaks of reddish blonde as was planned. But Joe, being a towhead already, had a huge surprise when he looked in the mirror. Evidently the

47

boys didn't take into consideration Joe's hair color. When they mixed the red dye with the whiteness of my son's hair, what else could they expect but a pretty shade of pink?" The audience responded in laughter once again. Everyone was amused, especially those students who remembered when Joe came to school a few days later. It was the beginning of many shades that Joe experimented with in the seventh grade, earning him the award for Craziest Hair.

Before he closed, Paul wanted to share one more precious memory. It was a poem that Dan had written to him in a Christmas card in 1999.

"This is a poem to my awesome dad Paul
Whom I will admire greatly forever
Whose deep blue passionate eyes entrance me
Whenever I happen to look into them
And whose face droops with disappointment
When I refuse to help him work
I have hurt you
Through selfishness and thoughtlessness
When all you have ever done is helped
You taught me to be a good person
How to laugh and have fun
I can remember when you would read to me or
When you called me PeeWee

For being short, as a young boy
Or the times when you would tease me
About liking girls
I hated those mockings when young
Now I laugh at my ignorance
I never like being away from you
I want to let you know how much
I appreciate your efforts
To make my life better, more pleasant
So I write this for love, for caring,
For teaching me the right way, for you
My honorable, one and only father

"'P.S. Dad, don't get too stressed out about life. Remember that God has a purpose for everything that happens'. He signed it simply, Dan."

Dan Scafidi's touching and very prophetic words echoed throughout the sanctuary, as fresh tears streamed down his parents' face. From where Ashley sat, everyone in the room appeared to be crying, too.

When Paul finished reading the poem, it took a few moments before he could continue. He gathered his thoughts, and then explained how proud he was that both of his boys knew Jesus Christ and that they were saved, something which would give him and his wife great comfort in the days ahead.

"Four days ago we were just like all of you," Paul said sadly. "Now, all of that has changed. Joan and I know that someday we will be together again with Daniel and Joseph in heaven, and somehow knowing this is what will get us through the next few weeks, months and, if God wills, even years."

> WHY AREN'T THEY ANGRY AND SCREAMING AT THE ONE THEY CALL GOD FOR ANSWERS TO THEIR LOSS?

Just knowing that their children were with God seemed to give Paul and Joan even more strength upon which to draw. Their faces were bright with anticipation, their eyes danced with hope, and an unexplainable sense of peace surrounded them. Ashley looked around the room again. It wasn't just she who noticed; it was for everyone to see.

Once again her confusion surfaced. "What do they mean the boys were 'saved'? Saved from what?" Ashley questioned silently. "And how can they be so confident about seeing them again? Besides, even if they do, what about now? I know they miss them. But why aren't they falling to pieces with grief and hopelessness? Why aren't they angry and screaming at the One they call God for answers to their loss?"

Ashley sat there in a world of her own, surrounded by sadness. Then suddenly she was pulled back to reality when the crowd started singing "Shout to the Lord" as the service came to a close. As she and her friends made their exit, Ashley's mind was spinning with more questions than ever before.

Joe Scafidi, 2001

Joe at home on New Year's Eve, 2000

Dan and his mother, Joan, during Honor Society
induction at Reno High School, 2000

Joe on a houseboat at
Shasta Lake, summer 2001

Joe sitting in the tent on his
last camping trip, August 2001

Joe and Dan cooking outdoors, August 2001

Dan's Reno High School graduation
with his parents, June 2001

Reno High School JV Cheer Squad 2001-2002
Ashley center bottom, Kara center top with Jenny
right and Cathy left. Other members (L to R):
Carly Mattingly, Elysia Oliver,
Meagan Foreman and Sara Miller

CHAPTER 6
FRIDAY,
DECEMBER 21, 2001
2:00 PM

The clock on the wall was moving far too slowly, or so it seemed. There were only thirty minutes left of her last class of the day on the last day of school before Christmas break. Ashley could hardly wait. But her thoughts kept going back to the memorial service. It was so touching and yet so unbelievable. Joe's gone. He's really gone, she kept telling herself. But her heart was still in denial.

Suddenly her thoughts were interrupted with the sound of the bell as it rang throughout the classrooms and down the hallways, and with it came the promise that winter break had finally arrived. Excitement and laughter filled the air, as the anxious students dashed to their lockers and cars to start the most anticipated vacation since the beginning of the school year. Two whole weeks of sleeping in, hanging out at the mall, going to movies, and heading for the slopes to ski, snowboard, or just play in the snow.

Ashley knew the next few weeks were going to be hard to get through, but she felt the time away from school was something she could definitely use. At least at home the memory of Joe's face and

> AT LEAST AT HOME THE MEMORY OF JOE'S FACE AND LAUGHTER WAS NOT IMBEDDED IN EVERY CORNER, AS A CONSTANT REMINDER THAT HE WAS NO LONGER OF THIS WORLD.

laughter was not imbedded in every corner, as a constant reminder that he was no longer of this world.

That evening, with a heavy heart and still many unanswered questions on her mind, Ashley turned off the lamp and crawled into bed. It was far too early for anyone to retire but especially a young teen on a Friday night.

Chapter 7
SATURDAY,
DECEMBER 22, 2001
5:30 PM

Kara was at Ashley's door right on time, and together they drove the five miles to the church on the hill. The Senior High Youth Group at Grace Community Church met every Wednesday and Saturday night, as well as on Sunday mornings. When they arrived, Kara took Ashley around the church campus introducing her to many of the students wandering the halls. Then the girls walked into the small building to the side of the main church where the high school group met. The students took their seats, and the room filled with noise and laughter. Kara and Ashley found a table near the back with two vacant chairs.

At exactly six o'clock the Senior High School Worship Team gathered on stage and began to play.

Everyone stood to sing praises to the Lord, as the words were flashed on the big screen above. Ashley joined in as the students clapped in time; raising their hands high in the air and giving praise to the One who is King. When they were through, the Senior High Youth Pastor, Tim Harvey, stepped to the front of the room. Because it was close to Christmas, it was fitting for Tim to talk about the birth of Jesus Christ. But he suddenly and unexpectedly decided to also talk of Christ's death and resurrection. As Tim got deeper into his message, Ashley watched and listened carefully, and her heart began to stir.

"John 3:16 tells us that God sent His only Son to earth, sacrificing Him on the cross so that we could live eternally with Him someday! Can you imagine the pain God must have felt watching His Son die?" he asked. "I don't know anyone that I would sacrifice my child's life for. Yet, God gave the world His Son so that we could be saved. Jesus died for our sins before we were ever born." Tim paused for a minute, allowing his words to sink in. Then he continued.

"Can you even imagine for one minute how much Jesus must have been hurting as He hung there on the cross waiting to die? He could have stopped it if He wanted to, you know. He definitely had the power. But

He didn't even try. Sin had to be paid for. Our sin. That's why He died, then rose again. It was for us, because He loves us that much! Is that incredible or what?" Tim said in a voice that cracked with emotion.

"As most of us know by now, it is not easy living here on earth in a world that belongs to Satan. But living here is even more difficult if we try to do it without God. We all need Him to help guide us and help us through the trials we have ahead. You might not have yet dealt with a lot of trials or struggles, but you will! And without the comfort of God's promise and strength, or His wisdom and love, we don't stand a chance." Tim spoke to the entire room, but Ashley felt the message was only intended for her.

She immediately thought of Joan and Paul. Was God really the reason for their strength, their peace of mind, and their faith? Was it in knowing God and that Jesus died for them? Could it be that simple?

When Tim was through and the last song was played, Kara took her friend over to him and introduced her.

> AND WITHOUT THE COMFORT OF GOD'S PROMISE AND STRENGTH, OR HIS WISDOM AND LOVE, WE DON'T STAND A CHANCE

Ashley had so many questions; she hardly knew where to begin. Tim was touched by the anxious heart of this teenager, who wanted to know all there was to know, and how to find the peace she so desperately needed after the loss of her friend.

"I just don't understand why Joe had to die. It seems so unfair," Ashley told Tim, as tears filled her eyes once again. "I'm so confused, because Joe's parents don't seem to feel as badly as I do. I mean, I know they feel terrible and they are very sad, but they are handling it so much better than I am. What do they know that I don't?"

"Jesus, Ashley. They know Jesus," he told her. "And they put all their trust in God. He gives them all the comfort they need right now, to help them through this unbelievable time of pain and suffering." The Scafidis were members of Grace Church and Tim knew them all very well.

"But that makes no sense to me. How can He be such a good God when people like Joe and his brother die so young and for no apparent reason?" Ashley wanted to know.

"We don't know why God lets things happen like what happened to Joe and Dan," he told her honestly. "But we do know that He never makes a mistake.

Never. God is perfect in everything He does. He knows us all and loves us more than we can ever imagine. Sometimes we won't know the reasons certain things happen until much later. There might even be some things we'll never know in our lifetime. But Joan and Paul trust God and the decision He made to take their children away to a much better place than here. Sure, it hurts them terribly because they miss their boys, but they trust God with all their hearts. They know that whatever the reason, someday this tragedy will be to glorify Him.

"In Isaiah 57:1–2 it says, *'Good men perish; and no one seems to care or wonder why. No one seems to realize that God is taking them away from evil days ahead. For the godly who die shall rest in peace.'* Death is sometimes God's way of taking people away from evil," Tim went on, hoping he was making sense. "From what kind of evil we don't know. Only God knows the reason. We do know that no one lives one day more or less than God intends. *'All the days planned for me were written in Your book before I was one day old.'* That's from Psalm 139:16. Or in James 4:14 where it says, *'You are like a mist that appears for a short time, but then goes away.'*

"In God's plan every life is long enough and every death is timely, even with kids. You and I wish that they had lived longer, but God knows better. Those who die know their life was as long as God wanted it to be, because they are the first to accept God's decision of death. While we mourn their loss and question God's motives, Joe and Dan are lifting their hands in worship and praise to Him." As Tim explained, both girls listened intently.

"I think it's starting to make a little sense," Ashley said. "I just can't believe how much this whole thing has affected me. I thought I knew who God was and that I was going to heaven with everyone else. But I wasn't even close." Ashley took a deep breath. Then she said sweetly, in a voice barely loud enough for Tim to hear. "I want to know what I can do to be more like them, like Joan and Paul. Can you help me?"

"What you need is to have Christ living inside of you and truly believe that He is your Savior," he told her matter–of–factly.

"What exactly does that mean?"

"It means if you truly believe in Jesus and what He did on the cross, He will save you from death. But not the kind of death that we all have to go through someday like what happened to Joe and Dan. It's the death caused by our sins and trying to live a life without Him. That death is being forever separated from God. Some people will die and never know Jesus. The closest they will ever get to heaven is right here on earth, as they watch a sunset or see a flower in bloom. These gifts that we take for granted everyday will never be known to them again after they die. For these non–believers they will live out their eternity in hell and in darkness, where there is pain and suffering forever. But for those who know God and believe that His Son Jesus died for them and lived again, they will have eternal life in heaven with peace and tranquility surrounding them always, where the sunsets are too magnificent to describe and the flowers bloom forever. In heaven there is no pain, no tears, no disease and no death. I can't even begin to tell you how wonderful it will be. I can only imagine." As the pastor spoke, a smile encompassed his lips as he envisioned his version of heaven and what it would be like for him someday.

"Life is so short when you think of eternity, Ashley," Tim went on. "Psalm 39:4–5 says that *'We are here but for a moment more. My life is no longer than my hand. My whole lifetime is but a moment to You.'* We might live for 70 or 80 years, maybe more, or in Dan and Joe's case it might only be 14 or 18 years. To us their lives seemed too short. But in reality when we compare any of the days we have here on earth to eternity, no one's life is very long. Our real life, the one God intended for us to have, doesn't even begin until we're dead and buried here on earth. But sadly for those who don't choose Christ, their death is only the beginning of a suffering never known to them before. And it will last forever."

"But if all it takes is believing, why doesn't everybody just do it so they can go to heaven?" she asked. "It seems easy enough and pretty simple too."

"Understanding it might be simple, but trying to follow God in Satan's world is never easy. Sometimes the temptation to do wrong is just too strong. I also think for the most part that people are unsure of what they can't see. And you can't see God, only the promise of Him. That's why we call it faith. We live by faith, Ashley. When He lives in our hearts, we feel it. But we also live in the flesh and in the world, meaning that we tend to do the wrong thing because it's easier and more natural. But it isn't in God's world. Someday we will all have to stand before Him and be accountable for our actions. Wouldn't it be comforting to know before you leave here that you will be spending eternity with the Father, instead of with Satan and the Hell he will call home someday?" Tim glanced over at Kara and smiled.

"Is that what being saved means?" Ashley asked, still unsure. "When Joan and Paul were talking about Joe and Dan at the memorial service, they said they were saved and they knew that they would all see each other again someday. Is that why they're so sure, because the boys knew Jesus too?"

"That's exactly what it means. Joe and Dan actually came to know Christ as their Savior when they were younger. Paul and Joan raised their kids to love and trust God, and to know the Gospel of Jesus Christ. Is it easy? No, Ashley, it is not. In fact, sometimes the hardest thing in the world is to remain focused and faithful and to resist temptation, especially when your life is turning upside down. But is the process to receive the gift of salvation simple? It certainly can be, if you understand and truly want what God has for you."

After a brief pause, Ashley took a deep breath and looked up into Tim eyes. "How can I be saved?" she asked.

"I thought you'd never ask. Romans 10:13 says, *'Anyone who calls upon the name of the Lord will be saved.'* Come with me. I will show you." Tim took her by the hand and Kara followed close behind.

The three of them walked to the front of the classroom and sat at the closest table near the entrance to Tim's office. With heads bowed, Tim began a simple prayer and Ashley repeated his words:

"Dear Lord,

Thank you for making me and loving me, even when I've ignored you and gone my own way. I realize I need you in my life and I am sorry for my sins. I ask you to forgive me. Thank you for dying on the cross for me. Please help me to understand it more. I want to follow you from now on. Please come into my life and make me a new person inside. I accept your gift of salvation. Please help me to grow now as a Christian. In Jesus name, Amen."

When they finished, Tim turned to Ashley and saw her tears once again. But her eyes were brighter and her face radiated with His love. He looked over at Kara, and she too was crying for her friend and her new walk for life.

"Are we done?" Ashley asked, as she looked up at Tim.

"That's it, we're all through, and the heavens are rejoicing and having a huge celebration with your new promise to Him."

"But how does God know for sure that I meant everything I said?" she questioned, not quite sure how it worked.

"Ashley, God knows His children's hearts, every one of them. He knows us all by name, every hair on our head. People can't fool Him with a promise they don't mean, even though some have tried. If your prayer was sincere and you follow the promise you made to Him, He has forgiven your sins and you will live with Him forever someday. You will never have anything to fear." Then Tim asked her, "So tell me, do you feel any different?"

"I feel like my whole body is lighter and this heavy burden has been lifted. It's almost like being reborn," she said excitedly.

"That's it! This process that you just went through is actually called being born–again, but obviously it's not like the first time. It's your heart and your spirit that have been reborn this time."

Tim stood and hugged both girls as he said goodbye. Then he walked inside his office. After he closed the door, he got down on his knees and thanked God for at least the hundredth time over the last three years that he had been the Youth Pastor at Grace Church, for giving him the strength and the words to do His work here on earth. Tim was always so amazed and so very grateful when he was allowed the privilege to bring another child to the Lord.

> BUT THEN THE HOLY SPIRIT REMINDS ME WHAT'S REALLY IMPORTANT AND THAT GOD MEANS MORE TO ME THAN ANYONE ELSE AROUND HERE DOES

Kara and Ashley left the church soon thereafter. As they drove home everything appeared so much clearer for the young teen.

"Kara, did you really feel any different after you were saved?" Ashley asked curiously.

"Oh my gosh, yes. I was so happy I cried. It felt like such a relief. With all the things I went through when I was younger—being abused and all, I felt everything bad had been taken away, and the guilt and terror was erased. It was such a cool feeling. And it still is, Ashley. I feel blessed everyday just knowing that God is with me. I know there isn't anything I can't do with Him in my life."

"It's going to be really weird at school, you know, just because no one will understand," Ashley said. "Does anyone ever give you a bad time, or tease you about your faith?"

"Oh sure. I get teased all the time," Kara told her honestly, "especially at school. Sometimes it's really hard to stay obedient and follow God because of the peer pressure and all the temptation that goes on there. It's especially hard when I see my friends doing things that I know are wrong. They look like they are having so much fun, and I'll admit that sometimes I want to join them. But then the Holy Spirit reminds me what's really important and that God means more to me than anyone else around here does. So I choose Him, and decide not to go with what would make me more popular!" As Kara waited for the light to change, she looked over at Ashley and smiled.

"I really want to do things the right way, but I know I'm not perfect. If I were I wouldn't need Jesus. I know, too, that I could possibly stray from His grace at times, because I am weak. Not in my beliefs, but in the world. I just pray that I am never too far away for Him to hear me when I come to Him and ask for His forgiveness once again!"

Deep in spiritual conversation, the drive home seemed quicker than usual and the girls suddenly found themselves in front of Ashley's house. As Ashley made her exit, her words touched Kara's heart.

"Thank you so much for taking me tonight and helping me to find my way. I understand Joan and Paul's strength now, and I am so happy that I will get to see Joe again someday. I'm very grateful. I love you. Oh and if it's okay, can I go with you tomorrow morning when you go to church? I really feel the need to be there," she asked as she leaned over to hug Kara.

"Of course you can come with me. I'll be here at eight. And you're welcome, but I didn't really do anything. God did it. Besides, what kind of a friend would I be if I didn't tell you about Jesus and at least try to keep you from going to hell? Think about that when you approach your other friends like Jenny and Cat. You want them in heaven with you, don't you, Ash? At least let them hear what you have to say. Then it's up to them. I'll see you tomorrow. Good night."

Chuck was waiting for her in the living room when she opened the door. He saw a different girl than the one who had left nearly three hours before. Ashley told her dad what had taken place at church, and although he didn't really understand her newfound joy, he certainly didn't object to it, either. Chuck knew that Ashley had been having difficulty dealing with the loss of her friend, and if whatever she experienced tonight helped her, it was fine with him. It felt good to have his daughter back again.

That night, while Ashley lay in bed looking out at the stars, she said a quiet prayer in hopes that He was listening once again.

"God, It's me, Ashley. As You know, I'm finally walking with Jesus and I am so grateful to You for showing me the way. I want to be all that You want and do all that I need to do in order to glorify Your name, Lord. Please help me to help others find their way to You. And Lord, please help me to be strong, like You made Joan and Paul, so I, too, can accept the death of my dear friend and know that he is safe in heaven with You. And if possible, Lord, could you please tell him hello for me and that I miss him and love him, and that I, too, will see him again someday? Thank you for Your love and Your gift of life. Amen."

Ashley slept better than she had in a week. She woke refreshed and ready to take on the world.

CHAPTER 8
SUNDAY,
DECEMBER 23, 2001
8:00 AM

The girls drove to the early Sunday service together.
They chose to go into the big church instead of
the youth group and they were glad they did. When
they walked into the sanctuary they noticed a large
crowd gathering at the front near the stage. When
they got closer they saw why. It was Joan and Paul.
Everyone was reaching out to them, trying to give their
condolences by hugging them and hopefully saying
something that might ease their pain. But what words
could there possibly be that would even come close?
This was the couple's first appearance in church since
their boys had been killed over a week ago.

As Ashley and Kara made their way toward
the stage, Joan looked up and caught the eyes of

her young friend. She smiled knowingly and reached out her arms. Ashley was drawn immediately into the warmth and comfort of one of the only other people who suffered more than she did.

> ASHLEY WAS DRAWN IMMEDIATELY INTO THE WARMTH AND COMFORT OF ONE OF THE ONLY OTHER PEOPLE WHO SUFFERED MORE THAN SHE DID

"I'm so glad you're here today," Joan said hugging Ashley tighter, as she smiled over at Kara. "This is going to be hard, but we felt it was necessary. Paul and I both had this incredible urge to come and hear the message."

After everyone had embraced, Kara leaned over and told both of them the news.

"I know your loss is still very painful and will be for a very long time. But there is something wonderful that has come out of it all. Because of what happened to Joe, Ashley was saved last night!"

Joan's eyes immediately filled with tears, and she and Paul had to muffle a happy cry.

"Oh thank God. I knew there had to be something good in all of this!" Joan said, as she hugged Ashley once again. "We are so happy for you, sweetie. What a gift you have given to us. Thank you!"

Then Paul held both girls tightly, sharing in the joy of the moment, as the words filled his heart.

"I would never have guessed that losing our children would bring salvation for someone else. But I suddenly realize what I want for all our pain and sacrifice. I want us to be instrumental in leading the lost souls of the world to know Jesus, especially the kids. And we won't settle for just one or two. Our children were worth much more than that. I want hundreds coming forward and confessing that Jesus is their Lord and Savior. If Joan and I could have that, then maybe we will be able to understand our loss better." Paul made no move to hide his feelings, as tears rolled down his cheeks.

After the service ended, everyone was drawn once again to the couple in the front row. They seemed to have the most amazing strength, more than any of them had ever witnessed. The people just couldn't get enough, as they continued to console and reach out to Paul and Joan in any way they could. Those in attendance knew that the Scafidi's days ahead would be harder than ever to accept and deal with the loss of their sons and loneliness that followed. It was Christmas, a time for children and families to be together. But Paul and Joan would not be celebrating this year, at least not as they had done for the past 18 years.

This year they never got around to putting up a Christmas tree. Now it didn't seem necessary. The few decorations that Joan had put up the week before had long sense been removed, and the early gifts they bought for their boys were given to their children's two closest friends whom they knew could use the new snowboard and tennis racket. For Joan and Paul, the only reminders of the Christmas season were the outside Christmas lights that hung from some of the neighbors' houses and trees. Other than that, it was like any other winter day, minus the disturbing sounds of silence that suddenly filled their once–happy home.

Later when they returned home from church, the couple tearfully went through their children's bedrooms, removing personal items, clothing, trophies and trinkets. They planned to remodel both bedrooms after Christmas, turning them into offices in hopes that their new appearance would also remove some of the bittersweet memories they held inside.

While rummaging through Joe's things they came across his Bible, the one they gave to him for Christmas just four years before. Joan let out a soft moan while thumbing through the slightly worn pages, noticing little earmarks where Joe's favorite Scriptures were, and seeing notes where he had written on the inside flaps and columns. She smiled suddenly when she saw how he had used M&M's candy wrappers as bookmarks. It was so like something Joe would do.

Joan clutched the book close to her chest and began to sob, rocking back and forth on her knees, as the indescribable emptiness ripped through her heart.

"Why them, Lord? Why take my boys, my sweet beautiful boys? I just don't understand! I loved them so much." Then she turned to her husband. "I miss them, Paul. What are we going to do? How are we ever going to do this without them?" Joan cried out, as she grabbed her stomach where the excruciating pain had surfaced once again, as it had done the night she heard that both of her children were dead.

Paul was immediately by her side trying his best to comfort her. They hugged each other tightly while attempting once again to make sense of it all. After many tears, they both stood and slowly began to compose themselves. Then suddenly it hit them.

"We need to give this to Ashley," Paul said, looking down at the Bible in Joan's hand. "It will help her in her new walk and maybe even bring someone else to know Christ."

"I was just thinking the same thing," Joan replied, as she wiped away her tears, feeling grateful for the distraction. It was as if God had planted the seed Himself.

"Why don't you wrap it up and we'll take it over in the morning before we leave for my parents'?" They wanted to be anywhere but in their own home on Christmas morning, and had made plans to visit Paul's family in California. "We can leave it on the porch. Then when she wakes up, it will be waiting for her," he said, anxious to have it done.

Joan went to get the wrapping paper while Paul wrote a short personal note inside the Bible. As they worked, they both envisioned Ashley's look of surprise when she saw the package sitting by her front door. It was another temporary distraction from the overwhelming pain they knew they would soon feel again. At dawn they would be dispersing half of what was left of their beautiful boys.

After their children were killed, Joan and Paul had them cremated, then mixed their ashes together into two separate containers. That morning one would be scattered at the top of Mt. Rose where the boys had spent their last day together. Ironically, Joe had told a friend earlier that day that when he died he wanted to have his ashes spread up there. With the container clasped tightly in their hands, Joan and Paul were flown

to the top of the mountain by Careflight pilot and family
friend, Dean Mischke, in order to fulfill Joe's request.
The rest of the ashes would be scattered two weeks
later at St. Mary's College in Northern California. That
would be for Dan.

CHAPTER 9
MONDAY,
DECEMBER 24, 2001
9:30 AM

The morning sun seemed especially bright as it peeked through the thin curtains covering her window and lighting up the bedroom walls. Ashley could have stayed in bed longer, but she wanted to do some last minute Christmas shopping. Jenny's mom was going to take the girls and drop them off at the mall at eleven. Ashley untangled herself from the sheet, rolled slowly out of bed and headed to the bathroom.

After she took a shower and dried her hair, Ashley made herself a quick piece of toast and got dressed. She was ready ten minutes early and decided to wait for Jenny outside. She opened the front door and walked down the sidewalk to the curb out in front. Though the air was cold, the sun felt good on her face. She hadn't been there long when she suddenly remembered that she left her money on the nightstand by her bed. As she ran up the walk, she noticed the package by the door. It was all decorated in bright Christmas wrap with a small note attached that read, "To Ashley, Merry Christmas. Love, Paul and Joan Scafidi."

When she got inside and opened it, Ashley began to cry. But for the first time in what seemed like years, her tears were happy ones. She held Joe's Bible tightly in her hands and ran to the phone. She had to tell Kara the news.

Kara answered on the second ring.

"Hey, it's me. Guess what I just found on my front porch?" Ashley asked excitedly.

"Did Santa bring you a present in the middle of the night? He's a little early and besides, isn't he supposed to use the chimney?" Kara teased.

"No, Kara, it's a Bible. It's Joe's Bible. Joan and Paul must have come by last night and left it on the doorstep. Listen to what they wrote inside. 'Dear Ashley, Joan and I were deeply affected tonight by your decision to follow Jesus. Tim said you asked all the right questions and we hope God will show you the answers you seek. Joseph cared a great deal for you.

This is the Bible that we gave him on Christmas Day 1997, to take his journey with Christ. He read it a lot and loved it. We know he would want you to have it for your journey. Thank you for your sweetness. We hope you will stay close to us even now. God bless you and Merry Christmas. Much Love, Paul and Joan.'

"Isn't that incredibly sweet? And guess what? It has all of Joe's notes inside and old M&M's wrappers to mark the pages. Isn't that just too cute?" Ashley was truly touched and felt so blessed by their incredibly unselfish act.

Most grieving parents would never have let go of such a personal treasure left behind by their son, but not Joan and Paul. They knew Ashley needed the Bible a lot more than they did. They also knew that she would use it to bring others to know Jesus, just as they intended to do for the rest of their lives, while they waited to join their children.

Paul and Joan knew the days ahead were going to be hard, sometimes even unbearable. But they also knew that with Jesus all things were

> BUT THEY ALSO KNEW THAT WITH JESUS ALL THINGS WERE POSSIBLE, EVEN THIS

possible, even this. And so they prayed once again for help through their sadness and heavy hearts, and to be able to understand someday what it all meant and why they were chosen to endure this unbelievable burden of pain and sacrifice.

Chapter 10
TUESDAY,
DECEMBER 25, 2001
CHRISTMAS DAY
9:00 PM

Ashley sat alone in her room reliving the events of the day. It was a good day for her and her family, as she remembered all the gifts that were exchanged, the laughter that filled the house and the gathering at the table for a memorable Christmas feast.

She gave thanks once again to the God who gave her life, for giving her such a wonderful family. But as she sat there, Ashley had a strange feeling that her day wasn't yet over. Her thoughts immediately went to Joe. She knew that her friend was celebrating firsthand, with the Host of all creation. But Joan and Paul were alone, with no one to say goodnight to, with no one to share neither their day nor the coming days ahead.

"How sad is that?" she said, while reaching across the bed and picking up the book off the nightstand.

"I can do all things through Christ who strengthens me," she said out loud. As she held Joe's Bible in her hand, remembering the Scripture from Philippians 4:13, Ashley knew what she had to do. The

> I CAN DO ALL THINGS THROUGH CHRIST WHO STRENGTHENS ME

time had finally come for her to tell her story, a story of loss, confusion, pain, and incredible sorrow and, through it all, how she found Jesus. Maybe it would lead others to know Him, too. It would be her gift to Paul, Joan and Dan, but especially to her dear sweet Joe.

Without a second thought, Ashley walked over to her computer and turned it on. Her heart–breaking story began with a letter:

Dear Paul and Joan,

I can't begin to thank you for all that you have done for me. I admire both of you so much for your incredible strength and faith in the Lord. I am finally at peace to know that it is He who has helped you through all of this, and that He will continue to be faithful and keep you strong.

I am not sure if you realize the impact you have had on my family and me, but I think it's important that you know. And so I write this letter to you, which will eventually begin my story of faith, hope, strength and courage, and the most amazing gift of all, eternal life.

When Joe died, I took it very hard. No one close to me had ever passed away before and the mere thought of never seeing Joe again brought me so much pain. But the youth pastor at Grace Church, Pastor Tim, told me that it is possible for me to see Joe again. All I had to do was believe in Jesus Christ, say the sinner's prayer and ask for forgiveness, confessing that He is Lord and that He died for me. That night I decided to become a Christian so that I could someday see my "Joey" again when I get to heaven. I know that he is there right now looking down on me, helping me to be a better Christian and waiting until I am able to join him.

Also, my dad noticed something special between you both. Though he didn't know what, something very apparent kept the two of you together and strong through this horrific ordeal. I told him that the something was Christ! He knew then that he wanted what you guys have together. He said he wanted to go with me the next time I go to church, which will be this Sunday. I pray that he does and that he continues to go, and that he and my whole family will someday know Jesus, too.

Paul and Joan, I want to thank you for everything: your kindness, your strength and Joe's Bible, but mostly I'd like to thank you for your precious sons, Joe and Dan. They touched so many lives, as you already know. And it's only the beginning. Many have found Jesus already, and many more will surely follow because of your incredible boys and the strength that holds you both together.

> MANY HAVE FOUND JESUS ALREADY, AND MANY MORE WILL SURELY FOLLOW BECAUSE OF YOUR INCREDIBLE BOYS AND THE STRENGTH THAT HOLDS YOU BOTH TOGETHER

I can't even begin to put into words what all of this has done for me. I owe all of you so much. Your incredibly tragic loss has led me to believe in Jesus Christ, and with Him I have found eternal salvation. I have been blessed in this life knowing your son, but until I see his face again and am able to thank him myself, I will thank you for being here with me and for your help in showing me the way.

This is the beginning of my story. I am grateful to both of you for allowing me to share it with whoever will listen, and to hopefully bring many others to know the Lord, because of your amazing sacrifice.

May God be with you and protect you always.

Your friend, Ashley Oliveira.

(Ashley's letter was just one of thousands of cards and letters sent to the Scafidis after the loss of their children.)

Chapter 11
SUNDAY,
MAY 19, 2002
9:30 PM

Dear Diary,

"I am so excited, I just had to tell you! Because of what happened to Joe and Dan, there have been so many students coming forward wanting what they had and finally confessing their love for Jesus. In fact, during basketball season, Jenna Wirshing, who plays on the Freshman Basketball Team and was already a Christian, started praying for her teammates. She knew they were not Christians and this concerned her deeply after Joe's death.

"Following the memorial service, she began to pray with her team before each game. At first there were only herself and two other girls. But by the end of the season the whole team, including the coach, was praying together. Several of the girls have even accepted Christ as their personal Savior. Jenna has been answering questions like crazy and always has her Bible with her so she can show them Scriptures!

> I KNOW IT'S JUST A MATTER OF TIME BEFORE THEY, TOO, WILL KNOW HIS LOVINGKINDNESS

"And finally, diary, I just have to share one more thing. My best friends, Jenny Luna and Cathy Strand, are finally starting to ask me questions about Jesus. I know it's just a matter of time before they, too, will know His lovingkindness. Then I will be totally secure in my heart that no matter what paths our lives take, or where the three of us end up in the future, someday we will all be together again in heaven. It's still going to take a great deal of patience and many more prayers, but I know that God will someday put His hand on all of it and just make it happen.

"Because of Joan and Paul and the unbelievable strength and courage they had throughout this whole tragic ordeal, all of these people who are coming forward realize that they want what the Scafidis have.

Even the adults, who see how strong Paul and Joan's marriage is because of their faith and trust in God, are taking the leap of faith. It's just so cool to see it all happen, and all because of Joe and Dan. It's truly a miracle. Without them even being here, they have already brought so many of their friends to salvation, along with dozens more they never even knew. But one day they will, when we are all in heaven together with our Father.

"I know I said once before that Joe and Dan's death seemed so senseless because of how young they both were when they died, and how much they could have done with their lives had they been given the chance. But now that I can see things better; it really wasn't senseless at all. In His perfect time and will, God used Joe and Dan in a different way and in a different world to help bring all these other people to know Jesus. I know, too, that God will continue to use them, and anyone else for that matter, until He has all His children with Him again. I am so grateful to be one of them. His love and grace are truly amazing. We are all so blessed.

"That's all I wanted to say for now, diary.
Until later …Ashley."

CHAPTER 12
ONE YEAR LATER:

Ashley Oliveira is currently a sophomore at Reno High School and is a member of the Varsity Cheer Squad along with Kara, Jenny and Cathy. She plans to go to college when she graduates in 2005, and promises to continue her crusade for Christ wherever she goes. She has become a frequent visitor at Joan and Paul Scafidi's home in Southwest Reno and a very important person in their lives, as are many of Joe and Dan's friends. The kids often hang out with them several times a week, watching football games, eating pizza, and playing cards and other games. The laughter and noise that these kids bring are like music to Joan and Paul's ears, as the sounds fill their home with joy once again.

The Scafidis have made it their mission to minister to their sons' friends, and often take dozens of them on camping, boating and hiking trips. They bond with them and are always on hand to teach them the Word, in case any of them ever want to know about Jesus. On several occasions, many of these kids have been

> THEY STILL WONDER WHY IT ALL HAD TO HAPPEN, BREAKING DOWN OCCASIONALLY AND PRAYING FOR STRENGTH CONSTANTLY

curious enough to ask, and some have even brought Jesus into their lives.

Paul and Joan know that nothing or anyone will ever replace their beloved children, but these gatherings help fill the void left by their sons' deaths. They have grown close to all of these kids and truly care about their wellbeing. Joan and Paul are extremely grateful and feel very blessed to have all of them in their lives.

They still wonder why it all had to happen, breaking down occasionally and praying for strength constantly. During a recent Bible study, Joan shared her story with the other ladies in attendance. She closed by saying, "I thought when you did everything the right way, bringing your children to know and love God, and putting all your trust in Him and His Son, that you would be exempted and protected from bad things happening. But that was not the case, as Paul and I found out. We still ask why and probably always will, but we are both determined to carry on, with great hope and obedience as the Lord continues to guide us through the weeks and months ahead."

The Scafidis have also taken up a new hobby to help them through their grieving process. Paul began taking flying lessons in March 2002, something he had never done before in his life. By the middle of August he had become a licensed pilot. In September they bought an older aircraft, a Mooney, and now spend much of their time flying around the countryside in hopes of distancing themselves from the memories they built with their children. Though the memories of Dan and Joe will always be cherished, the constant reminders of them have been too great to bear. These new memories will help Joan and Paul to live again in other ways, until they are once again reunited with their sons. They both look forward to that day with anxious hearts and open arms; until then they continue to pursue living for God and for His purpose.